THE PHILADELPHIA EAGLES

BY
MARK STEWART

New Hanover County Public Library
201 Chestnut Street
Wilmington, North Carolina 28401

NORWOODHOUSE PRESS
CHICAGO, ILLINOIS

Norwood House Press
P.O. Box 316598
Chicago, Illinois 60631

For information regarding Norwood House Press, please visit our website at:
www.norwoodhousepress.com or call 866-565-2900.

All photos courtesy of Getty Images except the following:
Icon SMI (4), Philadelphia Eagles (6), Bowman Gum Co. (7, 20, 29, 34 both, 42 top),
Black Book Partners (8, 10, 11, 14, 23, 25, 35 top right, 36, 37, 39, 43 both, 45),
Topps, Inc. (9, 21, 35 top left, 40), National Chicle (15), National Football League (17),
Author's Collection (28, 33, 42 bottom), Counterpoint, Inc. (41), Matt Richman (48).
Cover Photo: Icon SMI

The memorabilia and artifacts pictured in this book are presented for educational and informational purposes,
and come from the collection of the author.

Editor: Mike Kennedy
Designer: Ron Jaffe
Project Management: Black Book Partners, LLC.
Special thanks to Topps, Inc.

Library of Congress Cataloging-in-Publication Data

Stewart, Mark, 1960-
  The Philadelphia Eagles / by Mark Stewart.
    p. cm. -- (Team spirit)
  Includes bibliographical references and index.
  Summary: "A revised Team Spirit Football edition featuring the
Philadelphia Eagles that chronicles the history and accomplishments of the
team. Includes access to the Team Spirit website which provides additional
information and photos"--Provided by publisher.
  ISBN 978-1-59953-535-7 (library edition : alk. paper) --
  ISBN 978-1-60357-477-8 (ebook)
 1. Philadelphia Eagles (Football team)--History--Juvenile literature. I.
Title.
  GV956.P44S84 2012
  796.332'640974811--dc23
                                    2012016655

Manufactured in the United States of America in North Mankato, Minnesota.
205N—082012

COVER PHOTO: The Eagles sprint onto the field before a game in their stadium.

Table of Contents

ABOUT OUR GLOSSARY

In this book, there may be several words that you are reading for the first time. Some are sports words, some are new vocabulary words, and some are familiar words that are used in an unusual way. All of these words are defined on page 46. Throughout the book, sports words appear in **bold type**. Regular vocabulary words appear in ***bold italic type***.

Meet the Eagles

Football teams always like to make their fans feel like they are part of the family. In Philadelphia, everyone takes this idea very seriously. When the team is doing well, the fans act like loving parents toward the Eagles. When the team struggles, the fans don't hold back their criticism.

That kind of team spirit is why players love to play for Philadelphia. It gives them that little extra boost they need to make a game-changing play. It also provides them with the strength to keep going when their opponents are giving up.

This book tells the story of the Eagles. On game day in "Philly," the streets are awash in green jerseys, jackets, and caps. The fans are loud and proud, and they accept nothing but a full effort from the players, the coaches, and even the peanut vendors. That's fine as far as the Eagles are concerned. They wouldn't have it any other way.

Touchdown! LeSean McCoy celebrates a scoring play for the Eagles.

Glory Days

The idea of no football in Philadelphia might seem crazy to fans. After all, the city has been home to *professional* football for more than 100 years. But during the *Great Depression*, a team in Philadelphia called the Yellow Jackets actually went out of business. They were part of the **National Football League (NFL)**. In 1932, when the Yellow Jackets could not afford to pay their players or make repairs to their stadium, pro football in Philly disappeared!

A businessman named Bert Bell decided this situation would not do. In 1933, he started a new team and called it the Eagles. Bell hired his friend Lud Wray as Philadelphia's first coach. The star of the team was running back Swede Hanson, who had gone to college at nearby Temple University.

The Eagles were outscored 116–9 in their first three games and lost them all. When the team's poor play continued, Bell refused to give up. He believed the Eagles would win a championship one day. The other NFL owners had great respect for Bell. They later made him the league's *commissioner* in 1946.

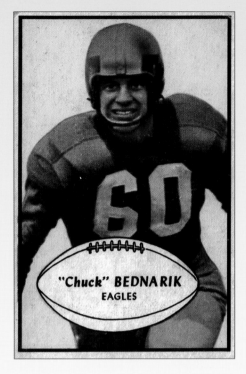

"Chuck" BEDNARIK
EAGLES

The Eagles soon developed into one of the NFL's top teams. They had the league's best defense and an explosive running back named Steve Van Buren. Other stars included quarterback Tommy Thompson, receiver Pete Pihos, and linemen Alex Wojciechowicz, Bucko Kilroy, and Al Wistert.

In 1947, Philadelphia played in its first **NFL Championship Game** and lost to the Chicago Cardinals. In 1948, the Eagles won their first championship in a rematch with Chicago. A year later, they defeated the Los Angeles Rams for their second title in a row. The Eagles wore the NFL crown again in 1960. Led by *veterans* Chuck Bednarik and Norm Van Brocklin, Philadelphia surprised the Green Bay Packers in a thrilling championship battle.

LEFT: Lineman Bucko Kilroy was one of the team's first stars.
ABOVE: Chuck Bednarik was a team leader during the 1950s.

In 1969, Leonard Tose bought the Eagles for $16.1 million. No one had ever spent that much money on a professional team in any sport. In 1976, Tose hired Dick Vermeil as his coach. Vermeil was an emotional leader who got the most out of his players. In 1980, quarterback Ron Jaworski and running back Wilbert Montgomery had great seasons, and the Eagles flew to the top of the **National Football Conference** (NFC). Unfortunately, they lost to the Oakland Raiders in **Super Bowl** XV.

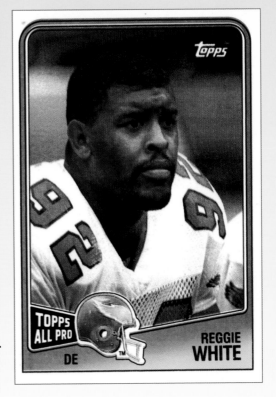

The team went through many ups and downs in the 1980s and 1990s. Some of the NFL's best players suited up for the Eagles during this time. Reggie White was an **All-Pro** defender who terrorized opposing quarterbacks. Randall Cunningham was a fast, athletic quarterback who was equally dangerous running and passing. Despite their contributions, Philadelphia could not get back to the Super Bowl.

LEFT: Randall Cunningham signals to the Philadelphia coaching staff.
ABOVE: Reggie White was nicknamed the "Minister of Defense."

The Eagles were eventually sold to Jeffrey Lurie. He was determined to bring the city another championship. In 1999, Lurie hired coach Andy Reid. The two plotted a **strategy** to help the Eagles soar again. One year later, the team **drafted** quarterback Donovan McNabb. He reminded many fans of Cunningham. Opposing teams had lots of trouble stopping McNabb, and the Eagles became a tough team to beat.

Philadelphia surrounded McNabb with a lot of talent. His favorite receivers included Chad Lewis and Terrell Owens. Duce Staley and Brian Westbrook were the team's best running backs. The Philadelphia defense starred Hugh Douglas, Jeremiah Trotter, Troy Vincent, Lito Sheppard, and Brian Dawkins.

McNabb led the Eagles to the **NFC Championship Game** each season from 2001 to 2004. They won the conference title once. The Eagles returned to the **playoffs** year after year, but as McNabb got older, the team decided it was time for a change.

In 2009, the Eagles signed Michael Vick as a backup to McNabb. Vick had been banned from the NFL for animal cruelty. He actually served time in prison. The Eagles believed Vick was a changed man and gave him a second chance.

Vick rewarded them with a fantastic season in 2010. He threw for 3,018 yards and 21 touchdowns. He also ran for 676 yards. The

Eagles won the **NFC East**. Vick got help from running back LeSean McCoy and receiver DeSean Jackson. In 2010, Jackson averaged more than 22 yards a catch. The following season, McCoy led the NFL with 20 touchdowns. The fans in Philadelphia love to root for a winner. They know it's only a matter of time before the Eagles are NFL champions.

LEFT: Yes! Donovan McNabb celebrates another touchdown pass.
ABOVE: Michael Vick looks over the defense.

For many years, the Eagles played in Veterans Stadium. It had a lot of history, but it was also old and outdated. In 2003, the team opened a new stadium. Everyone in Philadelphia loves it. They call it the "Linc." The players love the field, too. Their old stadium had *artificial turf* that was very hard. The field in the new stadium is grass, which is much softer.

The Eagles' stadium is great for fans because every seat has a good view of the field. If you miss a play, you can watch a replay on one of the stadium's two giant video screens. What's the coolest thing about the stadium? It might be the giant steel eagle *talons* that sit high atop one end.

BY THE NUMBERS

- The Eagles' stadium has 67,594 seats.
- The stadium cost $512 million to build.
- Mind your manners when you go to an Eagles game—the stadium has a mini-jail with four cells!

The Eagles' stadium is part of a big sports complex.

Dressed for Success

Most NFL fans know the Eagles for their green and white colors. However, their first uniforms were blue and white with bright yellow pants, in honor of Philadelphia's city colors. Bert Bell changed them because he got tired of hearing that his players were "yellow." Other teams used the term as an insult to say the Eagles were cowardly.

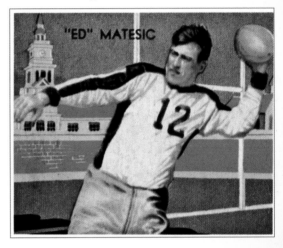

In the 1950s, the Eagles made another change when they added silver to their uniform and helmet. They also added eagle wings spreading across the sides of their helmet. The team uses a similar design to this day.

Like most NFL teams, the Eagles have uniforms that they save for special occasions. One version is a "throwback" to their old uniforms. Another features a lot of black.

LEFT: Brent Celek warms up in the team's road uniform.
ABOVE: Ed Matesic poses in the team's early blue and white jersey.

We Won!

T he road to a championship is never easy. It was particularly long and hard for the Eagles. After many losing seasons, they finally built a winning team during the 1940s. The first step in that journey came when the Eagles hired Alfred "Greasy" Neale to coach the team. Neale was very smart, and he demanded that his players give their best at all times.

Running back Steve Van Buren was Neale's favorite player. Van Buren was bigger than most linemen of his day. He was powerful and very fast. Neale also relied on quarterback Tommy Thompson, who was blind in one eye. If Thompson found a weakness in the opposing defense, he would wait for just the right moment to strike.

LEFT: Steve Van Buren tumbles through the snow and into the end zone.
RIGHT: The 1949 NFL Guide celebrates the team's 1948 championship.

In 1947, Philadelphia finished first in the NFL's **Eastern Division**. That earned the Eagles a chance to play the Chicago Cardinals for the league championship. They lost a thrilling game, 28–21.

The Eagles used that disappointment as *motivation*. In 1948, they became NFL champions for the first time. Philadelphia had a great defense that was at its best in big games. The Eagles met the Cardinals again for the league title, this time in a blinding snowstorm. Van Buren scored the only touchdown in a 7–0 victory.

The Eagles didn't slow down a bit in 1949. After another great season, they faced the Los Angeles Rams for the NFL championship. Again, the weather was terrible. A rainstorm turned the field into a mud puddle. It didn't bother Van Buren a bit. He ran through the muck for 196 yards, and the Eagles won, 14–0.

It was more than a decade before the Eagles returned to the championship game. In 1960, their coach was Buck Shaw.

His quarterback was Norm Van Brocklin, a great leader who was nearing the end of his playing days. Van Brocklin loved to throw the football. His favorite receivers were Tommy McDonald and Pete Retzlaff. They were dangerous on short passes, but Van Brocklin also liked to surprise the defense with long "bombs."

The heart of the Philadelphia defense was Chuck Bednarik. He had been a **rookie** on the championship team of 1949. Now he was one of the oldest players in the NFL. Bednarik played on defense as a linebacker and as a center on offense. He was the last true "two-way" player in football.

The Eagles met the Green Bay Packers for the NFL championship. Fans expected a tight defensive battle. Philadelphia led 10–6 at halftime, but the Packers scored at the beginning of the third quarter to take a 13–10 lead. Ted Dean got the *momentum* back for the Eagles when he returned the kickoff to the Green Bay 39-yard line.

Seven plays later, Dean carried the ball into the end zone to put Philadelphia ahead. The Packers made a furious comeback, but the Eagles held them off for a 17–13 victory. After the game, Van Brocklin and Shaw announced that they were retiring.

The Eagles played for the championship two more times, in Super Bowl XV and Super Bowl XXXIX. They lost both times. Still, Philadelphia fans will never give up. They remember the magical teams that won championships in the past, and every season they believe the Eagles will find that magic again.

LEFT: Norm Van Brocklin led the team to the 1960 title.   **ABOVE**: Brian Dawkins celebrates the victory that sent the Eagles to Super Bowl XXXIX.

GO-TO GUYS

To be a true star in the NFL, you need more than fast feet and a big body. You have to be a "go-to guy"—someone the coach wants on the field at the end of a big game. Eagles fans have had a lot to cheer about over the years, including these great stars …

THE PIONEERS

STEVE VAN BUREN

STEVE VAN BUREN Running Back

- Born: 12/28/1920
- Played for Team: 1944 to 1951

Steve Van Buren was nicknamed "Wham-Bam." He was one of the hardest men in history to tackle one-on-one. Van Buren was voted into the **Hall of Fame** in 1965.

PETE PIHOS   Receiver

- Born: 10/22/1923   • Died: 8/16/2011   • Played for Team: 1947 to 1955

Pete Pihos was a sure-handed receiver who was also a good blocker. He led the NFL in catches each year from 1953 to 1955. Pihos was named All-Pro five times.

CHUCK BEDNARIK Linebacker/Center

• BORN: 5/1/1925 • PLAYED FOR TEAM: 1949 TO 1962

Chuck Bednarik was one of the toughest players in NFL history. He was nicknamed "Concrete Charlie." He won two championships with the Eagles and was an All-Pro five times.

PETE RETZLAFF Receiver

• BORN: 8/21/1931 • PLAYED FOR TEAM: 1956 TO 1966

Pete Retzlaff played many different positions for the Eagles. His greatest value was as a tight end. He was an excellent blocker who could also get open on pass plays.

NORM VAN BROCKLIN Quarterback

• BORN: 3/15/1926 • DIED: 5/2/1983 • PLAYED FOR TEAM: 1958 TO 1960

In his three years with the Eagles, Norm Van Brocklin helped turn a losing team into NFL champions. He held players-only meetings every Monday morning so his teammates could discuss the previous day's game.

TOMMY McDONALD Receiver

• BORN: 7/26/1934

• PLAYED FOR TEAM: 1957 TO 1963

Tommy McDonald was only 5′ 9″, but he found clever ways to use his size to his advantage. In seven seasons in Philadelphia, he scored 67 touchdowns.

TOMMY
McDONALD
PHILA. EAGLES
HALFBACK

LEFT: Steve Van Buren
RIGHT: Tommy McDonald

HAROLD CARMICHAEL   Receiver

• BORN: 9/22/1949   • PLAYED FOR TEAM: 1971 TO 1983

At 6′ 8″, Harold Carmichael was one of the tallest receivers in football history—and one of the best. He ended his career as the Eagles' all-time leader in receptions (589), yards (8,978), and touchdowns (79).

WILBERT MONTGOMERY   Running Back

• BORN: 9/16/1954   • PLAYED FOR TEAM: 1977 TO 1984

Wilbert Montgomery could smash through the line for first downs or make long runs for touchdowns. He was one of the most feared and most respected players in the NFL.

REGGIE WHITE   Defensive End

• BORN: 12/19/1961   • DIED: 12/26/2004   • PLAYED FOR TEAM: 1985 TO 1992

Reggie White was bigger, stronger, faster, and quicker than anyone else at his position. It took two or three blockers to keep him from **sacking** the quarterback.

RANDALL CUNNINGHAM   Quarterback

• BORN: 3/27/1963   • PLAYED FOR TEAM: 1985 TO 1995

Randall Cunningham was one of the best athletes in NFL history. He could throw an 80-yard touchdown pass, run 80 yards for a touchdown, or punt the ball the 80 yards. In 1990, he threw 30 touchdown passes and ran for almost 1,000 yards.

DONOVAN McNABB   Quarterback

• BORN: 11/25/1976   • PLAYED FOR TEAM: 1999 TO 2009

The Eagles became a championship contender the day they made Donovan McNabb their starting quarterback. McNabb looked like a running back, and his arm was one of the strongest in the NFL. He set team records for career passing yards and touchdowns.

BRIAN WESTBROOK   Running Back

• BORN: 9/2/1979

• PLAYED FOR TEAM: 2002 TO 2009

Brian Westbrook drove opponents crazy. When they thought he was going to run the ball, he would catch a pass. When they expected him to go out for a pass, he would break off a long run. In 2007, Westbrook gained a total of more than 2,100 yards rushing and receiving.

LeSEAN McCOY   Running Back

• BORN: 7/12/1988   • FIRST YEAR WITH TEAM: 2009

An injury to Brian Westbrook opened the door for LeSean McCoy in his first NFL season. He went on to break the team record for yards by a rookie. McCoy was a smooth runner who made one tackler after another miss him.

RIGHT: Brian Westbrook

Calling the Shots

The Eagles have been fortunate over the years. They have had some of football's greatest coaches. Each brought a different skill to the sidelines, and each got the best out of his players in a different way.

When Greasy Neale took over the Eagles in 1941, NFL quarterbacks were passing the ball more than ever. Neale created a new formation called the "Eagle Defense." It took a player off the front line and moved him back into pass coverage. Soon every team in the league was using this strategy. By 1948, the Eagles were league champions.

Buck Shaw was a different kind of coach. In college, he played for coach Knute Rockne, one of the greatest minds in football history. Shaw learned a lot from Rockne. He got the Eagles to believe in themselves and play together as one. He turned a losing team into NFL champions.

Dick Vermeil depended on the leadership of key players to help the Eagles win. He built his defense around Bill Bergey and gave Ron Jaworski a lot of responsibility on offense. No one put more

Andy Reid watches his team practice. He coached the Eagles to four NFC title games in a row.

effort and emotion into coaching than Vermeil. Philadelphia fans loved him for it.

Andy Reid had more success than any Philadelphia coach. He led the Eagles to the NFC Championship Game four years in a row from 2001 to 2004. Reid built his game plan around the skills of quarterback Donovan McNabb. The Eagles were one of the league's best passing teams during this time. However, what made Philadelphia especially tough was its powerful pass-rushers and big, *agile* blockers. Under Reid, many of Philadelphia's victories were won "in the trenches" in ways that fans don't always see or appreciate.

One Great Day

Every NFL player starts the season the same way: dreaming of playing in the Super Bowl. For three years in a row—2001, 2002, and 2003—the Eagles came oh-so-close to reaching that goal. Each season, they advanced to the NFC Championship Game, and each time they lost. Philadelphia fans began to doubt that the Eagles would ever take that last, magical step.

In 2004, Philadelphia had the best record in the NFC. In their first playoff game, the Eagles defeated the Minnesota Vikings. Next, they found themselves in the championship game for the fourth year in a row. This time they would face the Atlanta Falcons and their dangerous quarterback, Michael Vick. A crowd of nearly 70,000 shivering fans took their seats in Philadelphia on a frigid, blustery day. The wind made the temperature feel like it was 5 degrees below zero.

The Eagles scored first on a touchdown by Dorsey Levens, but the Falcons stormed back and reached Philadelphia's 2-yard line.

Donovan McNabb celebrates the team's victory over the Atlanta Falcons with owner Jeffrey Lurie and coach Andy Reid.

Hollis Thomas saved the day when he sacked Vick, and the Falcons had to settle for a **field goal**. Each team scored a touchdown in the second quarter to make it 14–10 at halftime.

The Eagles were two quarters away from going to the Super Bowl. They opened the second half more determined than ever. The defense shut down Vick, and the offense controlled the ball with long scoring drives. Donovan McNabb was nearly perfect, and Atlanta could do nothing on offense. The final score was 27–10. The Eagles were NFC champions for the first time in 24 years!

Legend Has It

Did the Eagles once have a 30-year-old rookie?

LEGEND HAS IT that they did. In 1976, Vince Papale made the Eagles after a special tryout for coach Dick Vermeil. Papale was a track star in high school and college, but he did not play college football. Even at age 30, he was very fast and very tough. In 1978, the Eagles made Papale captain of their **special teams**. In 2006, Papale's story was made into the movie *Invincible*.

ABOVE: Vince Papale signed this photo with the word "Invincible."
RIGHT: Al Wistert was a star for the "Steagles."

Who was the best punter in team history?

LEGEND HAS IT that Randall Cunningham was—even though he was a quarterback! Most of the time, Cunningham used his strong legs to run with the ball. When Philadelphia's regular punter was hurt, he would also kick for the team. Cunningham's booming punts were legendary. In a 1989 game against the New York Giants, he launched one 91 yards. Five years later, he booted an 80-yarder against the Dallas Cowboys.

Did the Eagles ever join forces with another team?

LEGEND HAS IT that they did. During *World War II*, shortages of fuel and other resources—including players—created great challenges for NFL teams. In 1943, the Eagles and Pittsburgh Steelers agreed to form one team. Most fans called them the Steagles. The stars of the team were Al Wistert and Vic Sears. They would help

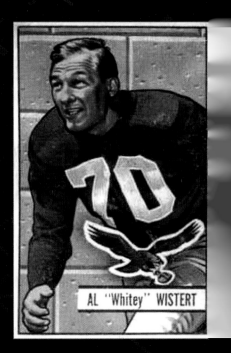

AL "Whitey" WISTERT

Philadelphia win a championship after the war. The Steagles won five games during their one NFL season.

It Really Happened

When the 1978 season began, Philadelphia fans prepared themselves for another disappointing year. The Eagles had not had a winning record since 1966. One of the few highlights of the year would be the game against the New York Giants on the Sunday before Thanksgiving. The two teams had a heated *rivalry*.

New York was in control most of the game. Joe Pisarcik threw a pair of touchdown passes, and the Giants added a field goal to take a 17–12 lead in the fourth quarter. New York appeared to have the game wrapped up. But with time running out, the Giants made a curious decision and called for a handoff to running back Larry Csonka.

The Eagles crowded the **line of scrimmage**. As the ball was snapped, Herman Edwards charged through an opening into the New York backfield. Meanwhile, Pisarcik bobbled the ball, which threw off his timing with Csonka. The two collided and the ball popped loose. Pisarcik tried to fall on it, but Edwards swooped in and scooped it up on one bounce. He ran into the end zone for the winning touchdown.

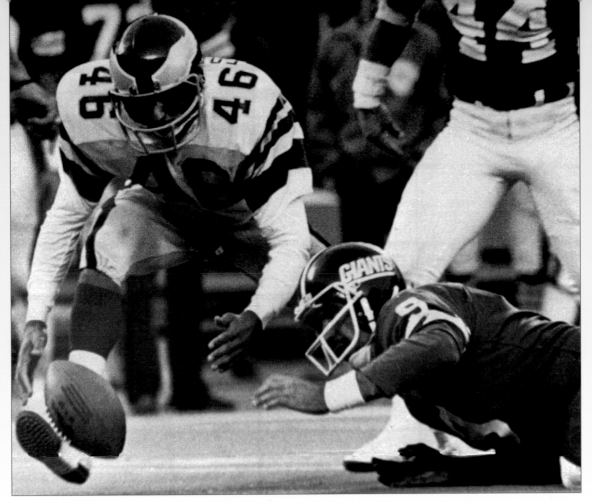

Herman Edwards follows the bouncing ball as Joe Pisarcik watches helplessly.

The victory became known as the "Miracle in the Meadowlands." The play gave Philadelphia a great boost of confidence. The Eagles played well the rest of the year and made the playoffs. Two years later, they went to the Super Bowl. Did one play change their fortunes? According to Edwards—who later became a coach in the NFL—it definitely did. "You're not worried about losing anymore," he said. "Now you're thinking about how you can win."

Team Spirit

Playing for the Eagles can be difficult at times. The people in the stands at Philadelphia games may be the most passionate fans in all of football. When the team is winning, the players are showered with love. When the team is losing, the fans really let them have it.

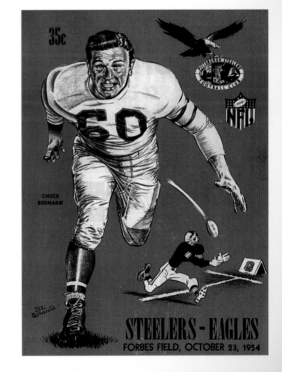

The Eagles want their fans to have fun at games. Their stadium has great views and an amazing sound system. The team mascot, Swoop the Eagle, is one of the most popular in the NFL. The Eagles' dance team entertains the fans during timeouts.

Of course, sometimes the fans make their own fun. In fact, Eagles fans are famous for the wild costumes they wear to games. Every Sunday, they try to outdo one another. Sometimes the competition in the stands is as fierce as it is on the field!

LEFT: Philadelphia football fans come up with some strange and wonderful ways to say "Go Eagles!"   **ABOVE**: Fans bought this game program, featuring Chuck Bednarik, for a 1954 game against the Pittsburgh Steelers.

Timeline

In this timeline, each Super Bowl is listed under the year it was played. Remember that the Super Bowl is held early in the year and is actually part of the previous season. For example, Super Bowl XLVI was played on February 5, 2012, but it was the championship of the 2011 NFL season.

1939
The Eagles play in the first televised NFL game.

1960
The Eagles beat the Green Bay Packers for the NFL championship.

1933
The Eagles play their first NFL season.

1948
The Eagles win their first NFL championship.

1949
The Eagles win their second NFL championship in a row.

Tommy Thompson (**LEFT**) and Pete Pihos (**RIGHT**) were stars of the 1948 and 1949 teams.

PETE PIHOS
PHILADELPHIA EAGLES

Harold Carmichael

Jeremiah Trotter starred for the 2005 team.

1973
Harold Carmichael leads the NFL with 67 pass receptions.

1990
Randall Cunningham is named NFL Player of the Year.

2005
The Eagles win their second NFC championship.

1962
Sonny Jurgensen leads the NFL in passing.

1981
The Eagles win their first NFC championship.

2011
Jason Babin has 18 sacks.

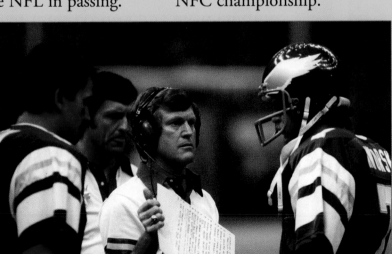

Dick Vermeil and Ron Jaworski talk during a 1980 game.

Fun Facts

OLD DOG, NEW TRICKS

In 1965, Pete Retzlaff won the Bert Bell Award as the NFL's top player. The 34-year-old tight end caught 66 passes for 1,190 yards

and 10 touchdowns. Not bad for a player who did not catch a single pass in college!

FAST FEET

DeSean Jackson was Philadelphia's most exciting player from 2008 to 2011. The superfast receiver scored 28 touchdowns during that period, including three on running plays and four on punt returns.

BRIGHT IDEA

During the 1930s, Philadelphia owner Bert Bell convinced other owners that the NFL would be a stronger league if the teams took turns selecting the top college players. In 1936, the NFL held its first draft. Ten years later, Bell was named NFL commissioner.

ABOVE: DeSean Jackson   **RIGHT**: David Akers

HOT FEET

One of the top kickers in team history was Tony Franklin, who played for the Eagles from 1979 to 1983. Franklin kicked barefoot—no matter how cold or muddy the field was. Philadelphia's best kicker was probably David Akers. He booted 294 field goals in 12 years with the Eagles.

NOW PLAYING IN D.C.

From 2000 to 2008, Jon Runyan was one of the NFL's top offensive linemen. After Runyan retired, he became a Congressman representing New Jersey. He was the fourth former NFL player elected to Congress.

SAFETY FIRST

In 1939, Philadelphia rookie Davey O'Brien led the NFL in passing. After the 1940 season—when the Eagles lost 10 of 11 games—he quit football to become an FBI agent. O'Brien said it was a safer job!

THREE STRAIGHT

Steve Van Buren led the NFL in rushing in 1947, 1948, and 1949. He was the first player in history to do this three years in a row. Only three players have matched Van Buren's feat since.

Talking Football

"Wilbert was superb!"
▶ **Bill Bergey,** *on teammate Wilbert Montgomery*

"The league is no stronger than its weakest link—I've been a weak link for so long that I should know!"
▶ **Bert Bell,** *on how he got the idea for the NFL draft*

"I never dropped a pass, period. A few might have gone over my head or something like that, but if the ball hit my hands, it was caught."

▶ **Pete Pihos,** *on his pass-catching skill*

ABOVE: Bert Bell (center) meets with other NFL owners.
RIGHT: Andy Reid

"I think it's important how we come together and how the **chemistry** develops."

► **Andy Reid,** *on the key to building a winning team*

"I did it because I knew how to. In sports, if you have the mental makeup, you can do it physically."

► **Chuck Bednarik,** *on being the NFL's last two-way player*

"I think the chance to play on a regular basis gave me a lot of confidence."

► **Brian Dawkins,** *on earning the trust of his coaches*

"There's only one thing that counts, and that's to win it all. If you don't, you're not a success."

► **Dick Vermeil,** *on the bottom line for coaches in the NFL*

Great Debates

People who root for the Eagles love to compare their favorite moments, teams, and players. Some debates have been going on for years! How would you settle these classic football arguments?

Chuck Bednarik was the Eagles' greatest defensive star ....

… because no one was meaner or tackled harder. Fans always see pictures of Bednarik playing center for the Eagles. But he was also an All-Pro linebacker. When opposing runners burst through a hole, Bednarik was usually there to stop them in their tracks. And when teams passed against Philadelphia, he was there to make a play. Bednarik had 20 **interceptions** in his career, including six in 1953!

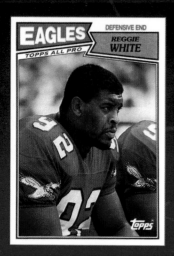

Not even close. Reggie White was Philly's best ....

… because he was the top defensive player in the NFL when he played for the Eagles. White (**LEFT**) was an All-Pro each year from 1986 to 1991. He had 124 sacks in eight seasons with the team and led the NFL twice in that category. In White's final five seasons in Philadelphia, the Eagles made the playoffs four times.

Donovan McNabb's 2004 Eagles Would Beat Ron Jaworski's 1980 Eagles ...

... because they were younger and faster. Speed is everything in the NFL, and the 2004 Eagles were quick at every position. No one on the 1980s team would be able to deal with McNabb, Terrell Owens, or Brian Westbrook. And Jaworski wouldn't complete a pass against Lito Sheppard and Brian Dawkins. They were just too fast.

Speed wouldn't beat the 1980 Eagles. They would win this game. ...

... because Wilbert Montgomery (RIGHT) would slice through the 2004 defense like a hot knife through butter. And speed wouldn't keep passes out of Harold Carmichael's hands. At 6′ 8″, Carmichael could reach balls that Sheppard and Dawkins would miss by a foot. And would speed keep Bill Bergey and Charlie Johnson from overpowering blockers and getting to McNabb and Westbrook? No way!

SPORTS QUARTERLY presents...

Who Will Play and WIN in Super Bowl XVI?
SEE PAGE 16

PROS FOOTBALL

FDC 55745
$2.00
FALL 1981

a LOPEZ publication

1981

Complete 1981 NFL Television Schedule

Los Angeles Rams: Once Again,Pat Haden Must Shepherd Them In

Pittsburgh Steelers: A Major Overhauling, or A Tuneup?

Buffalo Bills: Turning Things Around Without Going in Circles

Chicago Bears: Snap On the Chin Straps and Come Out Smokin'

San Diego Chargers: A Passing Game Known as 'Air Coryell'

Wilbert Montgomery
Philadelphia Eagles

Tampa Bay Buccaneers: There's Little Remorse, of Course, Around the Bay

Baltimore Colts: Plodding Along the Comeback Trail

The great Eagles teams and players have left their marks on the record books. These are the "best of the best" …

EAGLES AWARD WINNERS

WINNER	AWARD	YEAR
Greasy Neale	Coach of the Year	1948
Bobby Walston	Rookie of the Year	1951
Buck Shaw	Coach of the Year	1960
Norm Van Brocklin	Most Valuable Player	1960
Dick Vermeil	Coach of the Year	1979
Ron Jaworski	Most Valuable Player	1980
Reggie White	Defensive Player of the Year	1987
Randall Cunningham	Most Valuable Player	1988
Keith Jackson	Rookie of the Year	1988
Randall Cunningham	Most Valuable Player	1990
Reggie White	Defensive Player of the Year	1991
Ray Rhodes	Coach of the Year	1995
Andy Reid	Coach of the Year	2000
Andy Reid	Coach of the Year	2002

Bobby Walston

This pennant celebrates the team's first trip to the Super Bowl.

EAGLES ACHIEVEMENTS

ACHIEVEMENT	YEAR
NFL East Champions	1947
NFL Champions	1948
NFL Champions	1949
NFL Champions	1960
NFC East Champions	1980
NFC Champions	1980
NFC East Champions	1988
NFC East Champions	2001
NFC East Champions	2002
NFC East Champions	2003
NFC East Champions	2004
NFC Champions	2004
NFC East Champions	2006
NFC East Champions	2009
NFC East Champions	2010

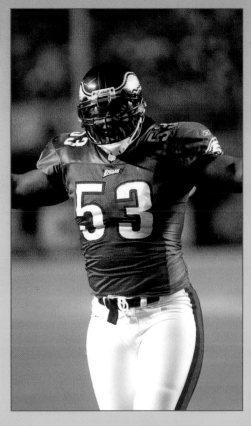

ABOVE: Hugh Douglas starred for the Eagles in 2001 and 2002.
LEFT: Asante Samuel starred for the 2009 champs.

T he history of a football team is made up of many smaller stories. These stories take place all over the map—not just in the city a team calls "home." Match the pushpins on these maps to the **Team Facts**, and you will begin to see the story of the Eagles unfold!

TEAM FACTS

1 Philadelphia, Pennsylvania—*The team has played here since 1933.*

2 Newport News, Virginia—*Michael Vick was born here.*

3 Parkersburg, West Virginia—*Greasy Neale was born here.*

4 Chattanooga, Tennessee—*Reggie White was born here.*

5 Chicago, Illinois—*Donovan McNabb was born here.*

6 Kalamazoo, Michigan—*Jason Babin was born here.*

7 Eagle Butte, South Dakota—*Norm Van Brocklin was born here.*

8 Roy, New Mexico—*Tommy McDonald was born here.*

9 Jacksonville, Florida—*Harold Carmichael was born here.*

10 New Orleans, Louisiana—*The Eagles played in Super Bowl XV here.*

11 Los Angeles, California—*The Eagles won the 1949 NFL championship here.*

12 Tela, Honduras—*Steve Van Buren was born here.*

Donovan McNabb

45

Glossary

Football Words
Vocabulary Words

AGILE—Quick and graceful.

ALL-PRO—An honor given to the best players at their positions at the end of each season.

ARTIFICIAL TURF—A playing surface made from fake grass.

CHEMISTRY—The ability of teammates to work together.

COMMISSIONER—The person in charge of a professional league.

DRAFTED—Chosen from a group of the best college players. The NFL draft is held each spring.

EASTERN DIVISION—A group of teams that play in the eastern part of the country.

FIELD GOAL—A goal from the field, kicked over the crossbar and between the goal posts. A field goal is worth three points.

GREAT DEPRESSION—The economic crisis that started in 1929 and lasted until the 1940s.

HALL OF FAME—The museum in Canton, Ohio, where football's greatest players are honored.

INTERCEPTIONS—Passes that are caught by the defensive team.

LINE OF SCRIMMAGE—The imaginary line that separates the offense and defense before each play begins.

MOMENTUM—Strength or force built up during movement.

MOTIVATION—Something that inspires a person or team to achieve a goal.

NATIONAL FOOTBALL CONFERENCE (NFC)—One of two groups of teams that make up the NFL.

NATIONAL FOOTBALL LEAGUE (NFL)—The league that started in 1920 and is still operating today.

NFC CHAMPIONSHIP GAME—The game played to determine which NFC team will go to the Super Bowl.

NFC EAST—A division for teams that play in the eastern part of the country.

NFL CHAMPIONSHIP GAME—The game played to decide the winner of the league each year from 1933 to 1969.

PLAYOFFS—The games played after the regular season to determine which teams play in the Super Bowl.

PROFESSIONAL—Paid to play.

RIVALRY—Extremely emotional compeition.

ROOKIE—A player in his first year.

SACKING—Tackling the quarterback behind the line of scrimmage.

SPECIAL TEAMS—The groups of players who take the field for punts, kickoffs, field goals, and extra points.

STRATEGY—A plan or method for succeeding.

SUPER BOWL—The championship of the NFL, played between the winners of the National Football Conference and American Football Conference.

TALONS—A bird of prey's claws.

VETERANS—Players with great experience.

WORLD WAR II—The war among the major powers of Europe, Asia, and North America that lasted from 1939 to 1945. The United States entered the war in 1941.

OVERTIME

TEAM SPIRIT introduces a great way to stay up to date with your team! Visit our **OVERTIME** link and get connected to the latest and greatest updates. **OVERTIME** serves as a young reader's ticket to an exclusive web page—with more stories, fun facts, team records, and photos of the Eagles. Content is updated during and after each season. The **OVERTIME** feature also enables readers to send comments and letters to the author! Log onto:

www.norwoodhousepress.com/library.aspx

and click on the tab: **TEAM SPIRIT** to access **OVERTIME**.

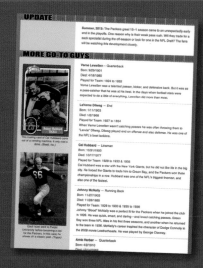

Read all the books in the series to learn more about professional sports. For a complete listing of the baseball, basketball, football, and hockey teams in the **TEAM SPIRIT** series, visit our website at:

www.norwoodhousepress.com/library.aspx

On the Road

PHILADELPHIA EAGLES
One Lincoln Financial Field Way
Philadelphia, Pennsylvania 19148
215-463-2500
www.philadelphiaeagles.com

THE PRO FOOTBALL HALL OF FAME
2121 George Halas Drive NW
Canton, Ohio 44708
330-456-8207
www.profootballhof.com

On the Bookshelf

To learn more about the sport of football, look for these books at your library or bookstore:

- Frederick, Shane. *The Best of Everything Football Book.* North Mankato, Minnesota: Capstone Press, 2011.

- Jacobs, Greg. *The Everything Kids' Football Book: The All-Time Greats, Legendary Teams, Today's Superstars—And Tips on Playing Like a Pro.* Avon, Massachusetts: Adams Media Corporation, 2010.

- Editors of *Sports Illustrated for Kids. 1st and 10: Top 10 Lists of Everything in Football.* New York, New York: Sports Illustrated Books, 2011.

Index

About the Author

MARK STEWART has written more than 50 books on football and over 150 sports books for kids. He grew up in New York City during the 1960s rooting for the Giants and Jets, and was lucky enough to meet players from both teams. Mark comes from a family of writers. His grandfather was Sunday Editor of *The New York Times,* and his mother was Articles Editor of *Ladies' Home Journal* and *McCall's.* Mark has profiled hundreds of athletes over the past 25 years. He has also written several books about his native New York and New Jersey, his home today. Mark is a graduate of Duke University, with a degree in history. He lives and works in a home overlooking Sandy Hook, New Jersey. You can contact Mark through the Norwood House Press website.

ML

9-15